JANE AND HER TIME TRAVELING BRACELET.

By Les McCloskey.

CONTENTS

Title Page

Introduction

Chapter 1. 2

Chapter 2. 5

Chapter 3. 8

Chapter 4. 12

Chapter 5. 17

Chapter. 6. 19

Chapter 7. 25

Chapter. 8. 32

Chapter. 9 36

Chapter. 10. 41

About The Author 44

Books By This Author 46

INTRODUCTION

This story has to start with Jane's Grandfather in the 1890s. It explains how and when the bracelets where made, then how and why Her Grandfather gave Jane the time-traveling bracelet.

Chapter. 1 Jane and her time-traveling bracelet.

Chapter. 2 Saving. The firstborn child.

Chapter. 3 The moonstones.

Chapter. 4 Explanation. How and why the tree of life works.

Chapter. 5 Matzos funeral.

Chapter. 6 The bracelet sends Jane on her first trip.

Chapter. 7 Donald Takes Jane Back to Africa to see the Tree of Life.

Chapter. 8 Jane went back in time for the first time.

Chapter. 9 Jane's time with the bracelet was coming to an end.

Chapter. 10 Facts about the BAOBAB Tree. The tree of life.

CHAPTER 1.

Jane and her time-traveling bracelet.

Grandfather Donald. Donald Patrick Rice, to give him his full name, was an explorer who traveled all over Africa in the year 1890. The reason he was in Africa was to study the African peoples and to send reports along with photographic evidence that supported his findings. Back to the Natural History Museum in Oxfordshire England, Donald had spent his early years studying the Origins of man at university, later taking a job working for The Natural History Museum. After working for the Museum for several years, the Museum asked Donald if he would go to Africa on behalf of the Museum. Charles Darwin had published a book many years earlier on the origin of species. Back in 1859. So this was the Museums way to prove or disprove Darwin's theories to their satisfaction. To this end, Donald had found himself in Africa. He had traveled all over Africa and studied numerous tribes. Sending back photographs and detailed reports on them all. He did the job so well the Museum had let his studies go on for years. Donald considered himself something of an expert in anything on the African man there tribal rituals and customs. Still, during one of his studies into a particular tribe he found, he became fascinated by them. Donald noted in his journals, the tribe worshipped an enormous tree, and they regarded this tree with such reverence above all others. The whole tribe became utterly devoted to it. They sang to it, made sacrifices to it, and held ceremonies around it. They carved effigies everywhere, depicting the tree in full bloom, Those people were a little known tribe called The Dogon, they lived mainly in south-eastern Mali high in the hills just south of the River Niger.

This tribe was one of the most dominant ethnic groups. They were also well known for making face masks and wooden sculptures, performing ritual dances, and worshipping the tree. Fascinated, Donald wanted to understand why these people would want to worship a tree and why they were so devoted to it. Though admittedly the tree was the most prominent tree for miles around, its trunk was fifty-two feet in circumference, with a large gaping hole in the truck, the tribe would use this hole to place sacred items inside for days or weeks at a time, though Donald was yet to ascertain why they did that. They called this tree the tree of life. Its real name is the Baobab tree. While studying the tribe, Donald had managed to befriend the shaman of the tribe, who's name was Matzos, a sort of a witch doctor. Also, the tribe's advisor in all matters, men, and women came to him to be healed when sick, or to have evil spirits chased away, because of this Matzos was one of the most respected men in the tribe. Even the chief would consult him at times of battle or for valuable advice. Matzos would take his lion skin bag from his hut and scatter its contents of ivory tablets all carved from the tusks of elephants.

The stone tablets then tossed into a circle prepared for this most symbolic of readings. The ivory tablets or stones were triangular, smooth on the top and the bottom. Both marked with symbols, engraved along all three edges each a quarter of an inch thick, the tablets depending on the face showing they could interpret either way up. Then by stacking the stones, one on top of each other, while maintaining the direction they landed. And reading the symbols on the sides of each stone from top to bottom, they could be interpreted by Matzos. Gathering the tablets from the nearest to himself, he would stack them reading them in the order, taking care to place each one in the direction they landed, by understanding the symbols, and interpreting them. Matzos could tell the chief what each symbol meant, give advice, or say to the tribal leader how a forthcoming battle would go, also what strategy he should use to defeat the enemy, even what the most likely outcome would be. This practice had proved to be remarkably correct time after time. Thus the tribe had become the strongest in that part of the savannah and the hills, so they had minimal problems with their neighbors, meaning they, for the large part, led a peaceful existence.

CHAPTER 2.

Saving. The firstborn child.

A little while ago Donald had saved the firstborn child from being attacked by a giant crocodile as she played at the water's edge of the river Niger, by jumping in and rescuing the child from certain death, he received a large bite to his leg, if it hadn't been for the tribe's men driving the crocodile off, he would have been eaten himself .his selfless act had saved the child and earned Donald the respect of the tribe, his leg had taken a long time to heal. Without regard for his safety, while protecting the child, he was rewarded the child herself gave Donald her half of a wooden bracelet along with her undying thanks. Don was moved into the shaman's hut so that he could be nursed back to full health. Matzos then adopted Donald as his son, and the whole tribe accepted him as a tribal member.

CHAPTER 2. 6

Matzos started to teach Donald the tribes history and innermost secret workings, like why they worshipped the tree of life and how it got its name. One of the chief's daughters had married the high priest a few years earlier and became pregnant because she was a princess and had married the tribe's holy man, the high priest. It made her a royal high priestess, the child she was carrying when born would be the most senior priest or priestess of all because the child had royal blood mixed with that of the priest's that would make the child very high born indeed. It turns out that the now heavily pregnant royal high priestess was out on the savannah gathering herbs. When a storm started, it came on so suddenly. It had caught her out in the open, and she began to go into labor. The only place to find shelter was under the big baobab tree. She had taken refuge at its base as the storm raged on. Her labor pains grew more robust. When a lion spotted her, it was running in to attack her when a lightning strike hit the tree. A burning branch fell from the tree, hitting and killing the lion, the lighting also split the trunk of the tree, making a hollow that grew and grew until the priestess found she could get inside the trunk of the tree and out of the rain, part of the branch close to the base of the tree was still alight. Hence, she pulled it inside, this kept her warm as she gave birth, her child was born safely within the shelter of the tree, she gave birth to a baby girl. (This child that was the one Donald saved from the crocodile). The child was known as the firstborn to the tree. After that, the tree blossomed instantaneously and produced fruit. Later the Royal High Priestess was found safe inside the tree, holding her newborn. When the tribe heard the story of how the tree had given up, it's a limb, to protect their royal high priestess and how it had split its trunk, to give their priestess a haven while bringing her child safely into this world. Then how the tree sprang miraculously into full fruit, the whole tribe fell to their knees and worshipped the tree from that day forth. From that day. Tribesmen and women gave the tree a name, and they call it the tree of life. Everyone worships it, the fallen trees limb now a sacred item was taken back to their village and given to the high priest. He put it in their holy place,

asking Matzos to take part of the limb and carve it, make something for the child to carry through life to remind her of the tree, Matzos did as asked, taking part in the branch and carving it into three parts. First, he cut a pair of bracelets, each so finely carved when joined together to become one. Second, he carved a box in which the bracelets were, kept. He then made the third part, a lid onto that he carefully cut every animal on to it, in the middle, he carved a copy of the bracelets.
Half of the bracelet.

The tribe so revered the tree. Gathering gems and jewels, that they polished then left in the trees hollow for up to two weeks. It shows respect for the tree. After that, the polished gems were taken to the tribe's holy place and blessed, then the jewels put into masks or symbolic carvings, or onto statues, idols and sculptures. They have even placed into belts or breastplates, all hand-carved with all of the animals known to the tribe. They were used in all the tribe's rituals or worn during ceremonies, rituals, and dances.

CHAPTER 3.

The moonstones.

One particular set of brilliantly transparent moonstones had been found and were offered to the tree then placed just inside the trunk for two weeks, but while they're in the tree, the tree was struck by lightning once again, and a red scar had formed through both moonstones,

The Moonstones.

no amount of polishing could remove the marks. The stones considered to be inferior. So they were given to the Matzos to do with as he pleased, the stones almost completely round. just a little larger than a garden pea, Matzos thought he could carve them into the bracelets, but found they would not attach no matter what he tried, so he drilled a hole into one of the bracelets just large enough to accommodate one of the stones, and placed the stone within the hole. Remarkably the wood closed itself encasing the stone within. At that point, the shaman put the carving down; he was so tired he went to his bed. The shaman had only finished one of the bracelets, on waking found that the second stone had attached itself to the other bracelet in the same way, and the carving which now also complete yet the shaman knew he had only carved the one. Only now both bracelets were finished, and the animals appeared to be running around the wearers wrist. The carving was so fine and intricate, far beyond anything Matzos could have done by himself. Now both bracelets, when put together fitted snugly within the box and the lid attached perfectly, Matzos tried on, one of the bracelets and found, even though they had been carved for a child to wear, it fitted him perfectly. Although when he tried to remove the bracelet, he could not get it off. That night after he had fallen asleep, he had the strangest of dreams. He found himself back in the village where he grew up. Stranger, still, he was able to talk to relatives he knew was no longer alive; they told him names and places from his childhood. The next morning he found that the bracelet was easy to remove, also when he told his mother about his dream, she told him everything he had heard and seen was true. How could this be he thought, so that night he put the bracelet on again only this time sat awake, this time knowing for certain, the bracelet had traveled back in time because he met an uncle who had passed away many many years ago. Yet, Matzos was able to talk to him. Matzos also knew it was time to pass the bracelet onto the child, but before he did he spoke to the priest, telling him about the bracelet's powers, the priest then took Matzos into the inner sanctum, deep within there holy place. Together they examined the bracelet. The high priest said to Matzos to protect my child do not give the bracelet to her just yet, not until you know it's full power just in case they are not safe. Only when you have all the answers and know they are safe, then and only then you may give one of them to my child, keep the other part of the bracelet and put the box and lid safely within the tree, the tree will keep it safe for the firstborn child. Matzos did as requested. Keeping the other part of the bracelet for himself while he studied it. He noticed that all the carving he had made on the first half of the bracelet had indeed reproduced the same carvings exactly on the other half of the bracelet, yet knowing he had only carved the one side. It didn't take him long to realize the limb from the tree of life had some kind of magical and mystical powers. As he slept that night he had a dream where the tree spoke to him it told him that the ivory tablets and the tree were linked and if he were to put the tablets with the symbol of the tree on the top off the stack, then put the tablet marked with the symbol of the moon directly underneath it. He would receive a vision telling him of the bracelet's mysteries, letting him know how to travel forward or backward in time. The tree also told him how and when the bracelet would relax its grip on the stone, allowing the stone to rotate. The direction the stone was allowed to turn, let its wearer travel that direction, being able to turn the stone backward let it's wearer travel back in time, or a forward rotation, let it's wearer travel forwards. A sideways movement meant it's wearer only traveled along his timeline. The shaman later found from time to time if the moonstone began to glow when he touched it. He found himself somewhere else, meeting a relative in need, only to return to the spot previously moved from a moment after leaving, even though he had been away for hours. These little diversions were spontaneous, and he had no control over them. Matzos named them his quickies. he found that by rubbing his thumb across the stone backward, he went back into his own passed. He recognized places and people from that time, or by running his thumb forwards across the stone, he quickly realized he traveled forwards in time. As he saw things well in advance of today, realizing he was able to travel through time, he spent the next few months rolling his thumb across the stone forwards and backward in the bracelet. He also realized he could only travel along his bloodline; in other words, he only met his relatives. He was unable to affect them directly, only influence their choices to change an outcome and so change their future or fortune. Also, he found he could not tell them about himself if he did nothing would happen to alter their future or past. Finally, he realized that he should never try to meet himself, from his passed or future, as that would change things that would happen to himself. Then Matzos thought he should start listening to the voices he had been hearing in his head each night, telling him who he was to meet and how to help them. Over the week's Matzos, using the bracelet was able to help many members of his direct relatives as he traveled backward and forward in time. Always returning just a few moments from the time he left, by now, after many many trips and good deeds, his tree in his mind's eye had started to blossom. That night as he listened to voices in his head, he was told his time with the bracelets was coming to an end and that he needed to find the next keeper of the bracelets, normally this would be a close relative. Still, Matzos didn't have any relatives that were young enough to take the bracelet. The tree told Matzos you would need to find someone with a good heart, with good honest values, the tree also told him you are going to live long enough to teach your choice of the keeper how the bracelet works before your vision tree is in full bloom and starting to form fruit on its self. Because Matzos had no living relatives of his own and was by now getting very old and sick, as he lay on his bed dying, the tree spoke to him in his dreams, telling him to chose someone with a good heart, That choice was easy for Matzos the one man he knew would fit the bill was (DONALD)

CHAPTER 4.

Explanation. How and why the tree of life works.

In the beginning. There was a void or a gap in the fabric of time that needed filling. It was chaotic. Nothing stood still. It was in constant turmoil in flux and changing. A gigantic cosmic storm prevailed for millions of years, then a consciousness came forward and proposed an answer, it suggested we need to calm the storms and give them some kind of balance because they are in a constant state of flux. What we need are careers to monitor and change bad things that have happened into good. Because for every bad thing that has happened or will, there has to be an opposite effect, so to balance things out, we need to even bad and good things out, at the moment there are far too many bad things happening all at the same time, resulting in all the storms. So the overseers introduced the carer system, many years later though the storms still raged on things were beginning to stabilize. Matzos, through the bracelet, became a carer, for everyone he helped by putting right something bad that had happened to them, the storms decreased a little. Very slowly over time, the cosmic storms began to stabilize. Matzos sent for his friend Donald. and over the next few days, he told Donald everything about the bracelets and the tablets. Plus, the secret of how to use it, he explained the meaning of the symbols Matzos taught Donald all he knew, then one night Matzos brought out a small lion skin bag. He said my friend, it is time for you to become enlightened, so I bring you your own set of the ancient symbols that will only speak to you, now sit by your home fire. At the same time, I give you the blessing that comes directly from the tree of life, with that he spread the new ivory stones before Donald and told him how to stack them, Matzos stacked them on the table he had brought with him, now please give me your bracelet the high priestess gave you I need to show you something. On giving Matzos his part of the bracelet, Matzos brought them together, and the two parts joined as one. Now please sit, there is a lot more for you to see, now cross your legs and rest your hands on your knees close your eyes, now think back till you can remember your childhood, and as many of your kinsfolk as you can, go back as far as you can. To help you, I have brought you a potion that will help you to recall. It will make you sleep then Matzos gave Donald a green drink from a gourd, Donald sat by the fire on a big animal fur and drifted off to sleep. After Donald had drunk the sleeping potion Matzos had given him, Donald had fallen into a deep sleep, the hut where Donald lay became dark with a thick mist. As it cleared, Donald became aware of a presence that spoke to him as he slept, Donald it said I am going to take you on a trip within your mind, you will, of course, be safe, by the end of it you will have an understanding of the talisman the child gave you and why. The talisman is in the form of your bracelet. It has stones in it, and depending on how you run your thumb across a stone will determine the direction you will travel. When you can move the stone within the bracelet, it will only turn in one direction, de-

CHAPTER 4.

pending on that direction the stone turns, will determine which way you travel from top to bottom will let you back in time. If the stone lets you rotate it from bottom to top, you will travel forward in time; however, if the stone will only rotate left or right, you will only travel in that direction and only within your present timeline. Running your thumb across will let you go left or right depending on the direction your thumb moves, or even rotating your thumb will let you turn in circles. Do you understand so far, (Donald nodded yes)? Now let me take you to the middle; it is where everything starts for you; this is your present time. The presence took him to what Donald could only describe as high up in the middle of a huge tree, we have to give you some idea of what it is your universe looks like to us and to give you something that you can relate to, so in this case, we chose a tree to help you with your understanding. Look around you. You are standing at the right in the center of your world. Or tree if you prefer, this represents your present-day life and time. From here, if you look below, you will see your past look above, and you see your future. Far below you, you will see lots of lights that are twinkling. Shall I explain them to you later? Yes, please Donald said, all around each light, you will see dust and mist twisting and turning that is something that is happening in your and their past. The mist and dust is the effect of putting something right in that timeline. You see, by changing one thing, it has a knock-on effect across your entire universe and their timelines and your's it is simply trying to stabilize itself. The reason for the mist you see, alter one thing the whole thing has to change instantly; this process we call balance. Balancing this is maintained by carers of which you are now one, each carer takes charge of their life in their past present and future, by repairing bad things that happen to others but only within their bloodlines, which is why we use a tree to explain how it all works. If you now look around you, you will see many many lights above and below each one is just like you and that's how they see you now, for every light you see an entente just like me takes charge of it, we guide you and them. We, in turn, answer to a higher form in this way we keep everything in order and balanced. It is your job to balance your world; it is ours to keep you all balanced. You will over time we will ask to travel backward and forward in time or even sideways to find a family member or relative that has had something bad happen to them. It will be your job to guide them to change something they did to alter the outcome. You will not be permitted to interfere directly; they must change things for themselves; your interference will change nothing; they need to do it for themselves. Your success will have an instant effect on your life as well as theirs; it will change instantly forever. You will see things you do not understand because, in your world, advancement in technology has not yet taken place. Anything you do see, you will not be permitted to bring back with you if you do, it will turn to dust as it does not exist yet; however, you will retain memories because you will see and hear things far in advance of your time. Now it is your turn to ask questions if you have any. Yes, please said Donald, how do I address you? What do I call you? I do not have a name; I am. Still, a thought or imagination, I may manifest myself as your conscious that's reminding you to do the right thing. You may feel my presence, but that is all, we are not human in the sense of the word as we do not need body shape or form, we are not affected by heat, light, rain, or wind, but we do react to turmoil, sadness, and sin. We are, in fact, in every living soul on your planet. It is just not everyone who listens to us. Our concerns manifest themselves as a thought or imagination. But we cannot affect you choice or will, that always remains under your control at all times, we only put thoughts into your head, it is in this way we strive to maintain balance within our realm. Every light you see around you is a carer that we constantly try to influence to put right a wrong that has affected balance; in doing so, our world becomes a little more even or level, henceforth I shall always be with you at all times in your mind. Helping and guiding you forwards by correcting your thoughts, will and does affect our common universe. Now it is time for you to awaken, from here on Matzos will guide you. When your time is starting to come to an end, you will see your tree of life begin to blossom and set fruit. It is at this point the name of your family member who is to succeed you will come to you in your dreams. Matzos had told Donald you only need a lure this person to come to you; to this end, I give you the blue vase of time he said. It will only pull the one who is supposed to succeed you to itself. It will draw them in like the great fishermen, filtering them out until it finds the person for whom it has been looking. When you find that person, you may lend them the bracelet to test if they have the correct genetic traces within your family tree to time travel using the bracelet. You may then give that person the drink that will send them into the dream state so that the entente can explain as I have with you telling them as I did with you, how the whole thing works. But for now, use your time to help your relatives throughout time, It wasn't so long after that Matzos took to his bed, he had been feeling tired and weak for some time, he told Donald that in his mind's eye he could see his tree of life in full bloom, so he knew his time was close. Donald spent every moment with Matzos at his bedside until Matzos finally passed away, but not before Matzos had told Donald that his gods had great plans for Donald they saw great things within him, then he closed his eyes as he whispered his last farewell.

CHAPTER 5.

Matzos funeral.

Matzos had the most lavish and respectful funeral that lasted three days. Then buried by the tree of life as was his request, saying he would like to be taken by the tree so that he would forever be part of it, The trees live for up to 5,000 years and reach up to 30 meters high, the trunk can reach a massive 50 meters in circumference. The tree trunk and leaves absorb water during the wet season, which sustains it throughout the dry season, they also grow all over Africa's arid land. They all produce fruit that stays on the tree taking six months to dry out completely after which the tribe can harvest them its found to contain healing properties, nutrient-rich seeds are ground down aid digestion and help with the immune system, it also clears and smooths the skin. Over the next few years, when the stone glowed, Donald had stacked his tablets as Matzos had shown him, and traveled back and forth along his bloodline meeting and helping the ones he had seen in his dreams. He had improved so many he had lost count; his relatives had lived long and happy lives. Thanks to the tree of life and the bracelets.

By now, Donald's tree had long since started to bloom, and his search had begun ten years before, but he had never found anyone to replace him until now that is, it came to him in a dream Jane Rice etched into his mind, he needed to find her. Then convince her to want to take over from him as his own time was coming to

CHAPTER 5.

an end. Jane's Grandpa Donald had spent some time watching Jane from a distance. He could tell she liked shopping with her friends, she was a happy girl likable and never shouted at anyone. Gave without wanting anything in return, never did a wrong turn to any of her friends or family, Donald saw himself in her, she never wished any harm to anybody, she would instead do them a right turn than a bad one. Donald set up a small test by pretending to be a beggar in the street just down the town from where Jane lived; she had even dropped a few coins into his begging bowl as she passed and wished him a happy day. It was enough to convince him Jane was the one. Donald knew if she was, in fact, the one, he needed to test her, how was he going to lend her the bracelet without her knowing what he was up too. Then it came to him, he had watched her for many weeks now and knew the kind of things Jane liked to do. What Donald needed was a shop of some sort that she would find interesting. He knew she wanted antiques he had seen her buy bits a bobs for herself, so with that in mind, Donald had taken this small shop in the back streets, placed the vase in the window as an attraction for her, knowing she would not be able to resist a closer look. On the fateful day, Donald had chosen to pass the bracelet to Jane; he cleverly put his plan into action. Jane thought it was her idea to go antique shopping that day, but Donald had sewn the seed in her mind days before when she had dropped the coins into his begging bowl. Jane had remarked on his dish, having found it unusual. It had some fascinating marks on it. Jane had asked him where he had bought it. He said in the old antique shop in the back street just down the road, telling her it had some fascinating stuff inside, and maybe she should check it out for herself. Thanking him, she left.

CHAPTER. 6.

The bracelet sends Jane on her first trip.

Jane didn't know what happened this morning. As far as she could tell, it was no different from any other day. Except she wasn't standing in her kitchen any-more, somehow things around her had changed, instead of seeing the things she normally saw around her kitchen like the kettle, a cup, the sink, a worktop, the microwave, a cooker. It was all gone, and she was no longer standing there. Instead, she was looking out over a vast empty valley, the grass was still green, trees swayed in the breeze their leaves full, and birds sang in trees, things somehow looked and felt sort of normal yet wasn't. She was completely disoriented and had no idea where she was or how she had got here. To her, things looked kind of normal but didn't. Something was off, and she should be standing in her kitchen, drinking a cup of coffee, not looking at this vista before her. Trying to clear her head, what happened to her this morning, what happened last night. Let me think she thought I got up just as I do every morning, hadn't done anything different used the bathroom, I washed and dressed normally, put the kettle on, sat on the kitchen stool, and read the newspaper and listen to the news on the radio. Then things changed; she could no longer hear the kettle boiling or the radio playing. She was here, but why, she started to panic and thinking she was losing her mind. Trying to clear her head, she remembered things that happened this morning. True enough and last week even, what she had been doing a couple of days ago, but to think back further, it wasn't clear. Hence, she started to backtrack in her mind, what was it that changed, she remembered catching the train and going into town food shopping on Friday, bringing it back and putting it away in the kitchen cupboards loading the fridge and popping the milk in. Nothing unusual there really, then on Saturday she went down the far side of town and looked around the antique centers just for something to do. I do remember the old beggar telling her of a shop somewhere down there and finding that very odd-looking shop down one of the back streets. She thought it must be the shop the old beggar man had been talking about, very drab looking it was too, just as the old beggar man had described. Still, that vase in the window had caught her eye, and she had gone in for a closer look, found that the shop was called Donald's Memories Odds Ends and what your heart desires. Interesting just as the old beggar had said. Jane remembered thinking what a strange name for a shop. But found the inside to be exciting and spent some time in there, just browsing. She bought a bracelet from the shop keeper a kindly looking man, she thought it would look good with her new outfit, just a bit of carved wood she thought, it had an unusual stone and the color of the wood it attracted her, or maybe it was the symbols marked on it that attracted her to it. She remembered the shop keeper saying something strange he said careful what you wish for, and he smiled at her funnily, then he shook my hand and said enjoy things to come, he put the bracelet into the very ornate box that had more symbols all over it. I thought the price he was asking for it very reasonable, so she had bought it, she hadn't thought much about it after that. Other than it would match any outfit that she chose to put on, funny that it really would go with anything. Didn't do much at all on Sunday, Monday she had gone to the cinema, then that was pretty much that, the rest of the week was quite mundane, with washing ironing cleaning the normal things I suppose she thought. That brings her to this week, last night she went out with her friends for a drink she wore her new clothes had done her hair, put on her normal jewelry and makeup O, yes the new bracelet she had put that on to show it off to her friends. I remember getting home in the early hours, and we went to the club, drinking, and dancing. Then I got up this morning, dressed and made a drink. Suddenly found herself hear? But where was this place? Good job she had put clothes on, she could have been standing here in the altogether. I have got to clear my mind, she thought and found out what is happening to me, she was panicking now, nothing made sense. Things with her friends last night went off very well they had a great time, they had talked and talked for hours about holidays, places Jane would like to visit, places they went to as a child and the wonderful times she had with family back then, reminiscing how good life was, it was perfect for her back then. In her mind's eye. She could see her Mum and Dad with aunt Charlotte and uncle Dan as she reminisced. Jane remembered playing in the stream with the rest of the children splashing about and chasing each other round and round the big old oak tree, what fun they had, she had been so happy growing up with her parents, it felt good to share her childhood memories with such good friends. That holiday must have been 20 years ago. When Mum and Dad were still alive. They probably still would be if that lorry hadn't smashed into them as they came to pick her up from school on that awful day. When her Mum and Dad had that accident that killed them both, the car had crashed into by the lorry; she wishes she could change things, so it had never happened, very upsetting losing her parents. After the funeral she had moved in with aunt Charlotte and uncle Dan, grew up with them until she moved to the city and started her new job as a librarian her mind had started wondering, she tried to focus. This place is strangely familiar. She could hear children laughing and playing just over the top of the hill. Jane started to walk up the small hill to have a look and to ask if they could throw some light on as to where she was. Reaching the top and looking down, she was completely in shock there in front of her not thirty feet away sat her Mum and Dad eating a picnic. Just as she had remembered and seen in her mind's eye the night before, she must have passed out because when she came round a cold handkerchief had been placed on her forehead and uncle Dan was saying I think she will be OK now it must be the sun's heat it's quite strong today. Opening her eyes, her Mum was holding her hand and patting it, asking, are you feeling better, dear, she said. Yes, thanks Mum she replied, clearly you're not yourself you called me Mum you will feel better in a little while, drink this it will help, and gave her some sweet tea from the flask she remembered so well as a child, it tasted wonderful just as she remembered. Sitting up her whole family were here with her, it was as if she was on holiday with them twenty years ago, her and her cousins playing in the stream, how could she be playing in the steam and be here as well, this must all be a dream. Her head was in a whirl. How could this possibly happen? Somehow she was back in her past, things coming back to you now dear her Mum said and gave her the most delicious hug she breathed in her mother's scent and perfume, being back in Mom's arms felt so wonderful, her Dad helped her back to her feet, and he hugged her as well, that felt so very very good. They asked her if she needed help or anything, she said I'm sorry, but I don't remember very much she said I think I'm lost, don't you worry dear, you come home with us until you remember things. Then maybe John can run you back home in the car, (John was her father's name) Can you remember your name, yes she said it's Jane, that's the same as our daughter she's called Jane as well? They packed up their picnic and gathered the children, and they all made their way back to uncle Dan's house just a short walk away, Jane knew every step of the way. She also remembered everything in uncle Dan's house. By now, she had stopped asking herself how this had happened or how Janes family got here jane. Jane hoped it would never end, how often do you get to see your family for a second time, she thought. she spent the whole afternoon talking non-stop to Mum and Dad and uncle and aunt they were amazed they had so much in common, but she couldn't tell them why or who she was, they would never understand, and it may well frighten them, later that afternoon. They made tea and sandwiches and asked her if she would like to wash before they eat, yes she had replied may I use the bathroom, with that jane went straight to the bathroom without asking the way, it's as if she knew the way to go said, aunt Charlotte. In the bathroom, she used the toilet, then went to wash her hands, took off her bracelet, and suddenly she was back in her kitchen. At this point Jane was freaking out, one minute she was at home in her kitchen the next she with Mum and Dad back in her memories some twenty years ago, then suddenly back in her kitchen again. Was she losing her mind? Her coffee was still hot from this morning she remembered making it before she had her memory trip, that was hours ago, it must have been a dream. But it felt so real. Behind her back, an oak leaf floated down from the ceiling but turned to dust before it landed on the countertop. Taking her coffee into the living room, she sat there trying to think about what had happened, picking up the phone, she rang her best friend, Sally. They had known each other since forever, they were at school together, told each other anything and everything, they were that close, the phone rang twice before Sally answered, hello Jane how are you she asked, Jane's number comes up on her phone, so Sally knew who was calling. Sally can we meet I need to talk to you please said Jane, yes, of course, we can, you know that Sally said, where do you want to meet and what time, how about Bernie's coffee shop around twelve I asked, I'll be their Sally said, hope you've got some gossip for me about the boys we met last night. Five to twelve Jane sat in Bernie's cradling a cup of coffee, dead on twelve the coffee shop door opened and in bounced Sally full of life and grinning from ear to ear, well come on then tell what happened between you and that boy Jason last night. Nothing, nothing. It's not that I need to talk to you about; something happened this morning that I cannot explain, and it's got me freaked out. Sally held her hand, squeezed it softly, and said you look upset what's wrong, tell me I'm here for you. Jane tells Sally about the bracelet. You know we went out last night, and I wore my new outfit, yes I do Sally said, you looked fabulous everything matched and you coordinated from head to foot. That's not what I wanted to tell you. I only wanted to remind you, do you remember me showing you and the gang my new bracelet with the unusual stone in it and the color of the wood. Yes, why? Asked Sally. You remember we talked about my Mum and Dad, uncle and aunt, and the holidays we took as a child. How I cried as I was telling you about my parents passing, yes course I do say, Sally, Why ? (Jane went quiet for a minute or two) Sally shook her back into the moment and said again Why ? tell me. Well, I relived my memories this morning. What, like a daydream, asked Sally. No, not like a daydream, in reality as if I was there, said Jane. You know at the picnic with Mum and Dad I was telling you about, with my Mum and Dad, Uncle Dan and aunty Charlotte, not only that my cousins and I playing in the stream, it was just like looking at my past happening right in front of me at that very moment in time. Yet I was there in person. I think I'm losing my mind, I went back to uncle Dan's place and was about to have tea, went to wash my hands took my bracelet off and woosh I was back in my kitchen, and my coffee that I had made earlier was still hot, but I was away for what seemed like hours, do you think I'm going mad. Sally hugged her tightly for a while, then sat back down opposite her and said Jane I just think you have been working too hard at the library long hours and late nights than out all night dancing drinking its bound to take its toll on you, fatigue and tiredness can do the strangest of things. Imagination can play around with your mind. But said Jane, it was so real and I think it's something to do with that bracelet. They sat and chatted for the next hour or so, and Jane put the bracelet to the back of her mind as they sat and drank their coffees and put the world to rights.

CHAPTER 7.

Donald Takes Jane Back to Africa to see the Tree of Life.

Now let me take you back to the place where the bracelet came from and show you the tree of life so that you can understand its power and blessings. But before I do, I need to explain a few things. After that l will show you how to use it. But for you to be able to use the bracelet to its full potential. You need to understand as many of the symbols on the tablets as possible. Because only then will you be able to travel through time, not only forwards and backward in time but also sideways along your bloodline, this enables you to visit any of your relatives. I draw your attention to the bracelet, you will notice the moonstone within the bracelet, but only when the stone glows depending on the direction you run your thumb across it, it will transport you as far into your past or future as it needs to. When it stops, you will meet your relative or relatives. After that, you will meet your family member; you are to help or put right a wrong that happened to them in there passed. The thing is your ancestry tree has many branches each leading to and from your kin, any one of those may need your help to repair their past, in other words, put something right that went wrong that was no fault of their own, but with your guidance, they can prevent it ever happening. they must put it right themselves, without your direct interference, but you can guide them into making the correct choice that will stop or prevent what happened in there passed that gave them grief or pain, by say preventing a loved one from dying before their time, just like your Mum and Dad. There are rules, though. You cannot tell them who you are, and you cannot interfere directly; they have to change their destiny by changing something to alter the outcome and change their future. Do you see what I mean? In a moment, I will rub the stone within the bracelet that will take us back in time to the place where it all began and teach you the meaning of the stone tablets and the symbols. The meaning of the symbols was taught to me by Matzos, the shaman when the moon was at its highest on a midsummer night, and he turned up at my hut with a small lion skin bag for me. Plus, a lure to attract my successor when it becomes my time to pass on the bracelet. To this end, he gave me the blue vase of time. It only pulls the one that is supposed to succeed me to itself. (This is where you come in Jane) When it found you, The tree told me to lend you the bracelet to test you to see if you have the correct genetic traces within our family tree, and to time travel using the bracelet. As you now know, I have tested you. Yes, you do possess the correct Gene, It is time to move on to the next step because my tree has long since started to bloom. My search had begun ten years ago, but I had never found anyone to replace me until now, your name Jane Rice came to me and etched into my mind through my dreams. What I need to do is to get you to want to take over this great gift given to me by the tree, as my own time is coming to an end. In doing so, it would ensure the good fortune of our bloodline. From the past and well into the future. With that, Donald reached forward and rubbed the bracelet on Jane's wrist, the room they sat in disappeared, and they found themselves sat in Donald hut back in Africa. Firstly he took Jane to the tree of life to get its blessing, then took her back to his hut sat her down. Took out his lion skin bag and tipped out the ivory tablets, saying to her, depending on the order the tablets land. What edges are facing you or if it is a wet or dry day or time of year phases of the moon and what time of day or night you traveled all will have an effect even the order you stack the stones. After that, you will receive a vision in your dream telling you who you will meet or if they are a male or female member of your bloodline. Also, their name and what it is they need to change, it will be up to you as to how you go about influencing them to do something different to change their destiny. That is the most basic way I can explain how the bracelet works, the marks on the box and bracelet correspond to the symbols carved on the shaman stones in my lion skin bag, these you must learn them for your self to use the bracelet to its full effect. Matzo, the shaman, gave me the stones in my bag. They are ivory chips, three-sided with a symbol on each side. On the top and bottom, depending on the side the ivory tablets land, they must be stacked in the direction they landed. The symbol with the tree must always be on the top, next under that, the one with the moon on it, then starting closest to yourself stack the stones in order, remembering to place the tree and the moon at the very top. Then by reading the sides of the stones from top to bottom. Then turning the stone to the next side, read that from top to bottom, and finally, turn to the far side and read that. You will then be able to interpret there meaning; the last stone tells you the name of the person you are to help, so you see there are infinite possibilities, the order the stones land decide male or female. But not until the moonstone begins to glow and you run your thumb across the moonstone in the bracelet only then, you travel only returning when you remove the bracelet or your task complete. Let me show you the shamans stones, Donald emptied the stones into the ritual circle. Jane began to count them twenty in all with three sides making sixty symbols to learn. That was the only that way up; if they landed on the other side up the symbol read differently. Each stone had a top and a bottom; the readings were different, so sixty became one hundred and twenty with twenty tops and twenty bottom sides. Jane looked at Donald and said, how do you expect me to learn all of those. I will need to give you the sleeping potion the same as my shaman gave to me and call your ancestors to help you understand the stones and their symbols, teach you how to interpret and use them. Let me explain how this works, the first time Matzo my shaman sent me back to my aunty Beatrice living in England ten years before I left for Africa, the bracelet let me spend nearly a week with her, she didn't know I had time traveled to her she just thought I was visiting. The bracelet brought me back and I found myself back in Africa with my friend the shaman, not many minutes from the time I had left him, when I had time travelled to my Aunt, Matzo my shaman sat me down and explained how the bracelet worked also what the symbols meant at the time, and why I could only travel along my bloodline and only to guide my family member towards putting something right in order to correct their passed, then they could lead a happy life, on completion the bracelet and its case would return me to where I started, having done it duty if you see what I mean, in this way I could lend the bracelet out to do good when finished its task it comes back to me, the thing is though I got to meet family from my passed and future, As my time is coming to an end soon I need to find the next owner of the bracelet that has the truest blood line to my own and has a good heart to look after the bracelet, then to show them how it can help the family for years and years to come, to this end it found you, Jane, now I need to teach you how to use the bracelet and how to pass it on when your time comes to an end, also I need to show you how to use the ivory stones and how to stack them, then I will give you the blue vase and the ivory stones that will bring forth the one you need to pass the bracelet on to. if you fail it, the bracelet will turn to dust and be lost forever. When your time comes to pass the bracelet on, you will need to show them how to use the ivory stones, give them the bracelet and the vase plus the tablets, then put them through the big sleep for them to be able to understand. After that I will send you back to your Mum and Dad and suggest how to go about changing the circumstances that cost them their lives, without forcing them to do your will, they must change things for themselves. You can only make suggestions they must choose, not you. Finally, never try to meet yourself or interfere with your own life, because things will change for you and you never get to see the bracelet or help any of your family. Do you understand? Yes said, Jane. With that. Ernest gave Jane the potion that let her sleep while Ernest invoked his ancestors to help Jane through her dream time. On waking, Jane was full of questions that only her Grandpa could answer for her now. Let me show you how the stones work first, and then I can show you how to stake them, and how to get your visions, after that we can start to look at your own family's past, and see how we may be able to help put it right. Are you still with me, and do you want to take care of the bracelet for the future now that you have seen what it can do ?. Yes, I would like that very much said Jane, will I be able to prevent Mum and Dad's deaths, Not directly, but yes if you make the right suggestions that alter things they do, like not getting into that car the day the lorry hit them. But don't worry, you can go back to them as many times as needed to put things right. Let us see do you remember the date it happened to them and what car they were driving. Yes said Jane the date was the day before my ninth birthday and the car was an old black ford, OK then said her Grandpa, you need to wait until the stone starts to glow then roll the stone backward in the bracelet it will know when to stop. It will bring you back when it has completed its task; you may need a few attempts before you get the desired effect; you are still learning. As soon as the stone began to glow, Jane spun the stone backward, and instantly she was transported back to her Mum and Dad she met them in the village just coming out of the church. Nice to see you again, Jane. Her mother said what happened to you. You just shot off forgetting to say bye, yes I'm sorry I remembered it came back to me so suddenly. I needed to get home quickly, sorry, not to worry, told her Mum you're here now that's all that matters, glad to see your OK. Jane had traveled back to see her Mum two days before the accident had happened; it was the day of her birthday. She would be nine that day. It should have been such a happy day. Then that stupid accident, how was Jane going to change things so that Mum and Dad never got into the car, Jane had a plan, she would let the tires down an hour before they were due to leave to pick her up from school, she thought Mum would ask uncle Dan to come and pick Jane up from school that day and everything would be alright. Unfortunately, when she had let all the air out of the tires, she took the bracelet off and returned to her Grandfather. What she hadn't realized was that her Dad had a compressor in his garage, he had found the tires flat thought that kids were playing about and reinflated them, he would still have time to make it to the school. Jane realized nothing had changed as soon as she met her Grandfather she broke down crying, I failed now I will never get them back. Now Jane, don't upset yourself, her Grandfather said you didn't think it through, you tried to put things right yourself, but don't worry, you simply have to think of another way, that's all. The tree and the bracelet know you have to learn how to use them so you will be able to go back and try again. What you mean given a second chance asked Jane. Yes he said, but that won't always be the case, so you need to think before you do something that you think will make them do something different, but if you've interfered nothing changes, so think hard before you go back, is there anything that someone else can do to change the outcome. Jane sat and thought for hours; then it came to her in a blinding flash. She couldn't do anything herself now, but back then, she knew how much her parents loved Jane and would make sure she looked after if she became ill, they would keep her at home until she was better. She racked her brain, think there has to be something. I know chocolate? Jane loves chocolate, that chocolate that gives you diarrhea, if I got some of that made it into hand made chocolates and put them in a box for the child Jane, I know Mum would give the child a couple of chocolates after tea. Jane could sneak back and change the rest of the chocolates, for milk chocolates before anyone found out. That way, she had not directly given the chocolates to the child or made her mother do it. If Jane had a bad case of diarrhea, Mum would ring the school and tell them that Jane would not be in that day. And would send a doctors note. It should only give Jane a mild tummy upset and a little discomfort. But it would be worth it, So Jane went off to the chemist bought the chocolate she needed and made the sweets put them in a small cardboard box, then went back in time to deliver them. Her mother said how thoughtful. I will let Jane have them after tea. It is her birthday tomorrow so she can have a little treat later after Jane had watched the child have a couple of the sweets she quickly changed the rest for milk chocolates as planned, it worked Jane did not attend school, her parents never went to pick her up, and the accident never happened. Jane's life changed in an instant she had grown up in the family home, her Mum and Dad lived to be a ripe old age, Jane went to visit them every week as by then she had moved to town for work and had got her flat. Hugging her Grandfather and saying will it always be like this, you know helping people to put things right. Yes, he said you have a charmed life now, you can help so many. But all ways remember to think before you act and you will do so much good your reward will come when the tree calls you at the end of your time when it starts to blossom it will be your time to find a replacement to look after the bracelet. When your tree is in full fruit, it will be time to pass the bracelet on to your chosen one. When her grandfather passed away, she watched while he was as his shaman had been before him, Donald laid to rest under the tree of life. What a life she was going to lead, she was truly blessed.

CHAPTER. 8.

Jane went back in time for the first time.

The first time Jane was given a vision, she was sitting with her friend Sally in her favorite cafe Bernie's, it came over her so suddenly, a relative, a child, had a boating accident of sorts. He and a friend had built a raft. He was alone on the lake when it clap-sized, and he drowned. Jane knew she needed to help. She knew she could not directly stop the lad, so she had to think of a way to stop him from ever getting on that raft. First, she thought what if I simply untied the raft and set it adrift, but she knew if she did that, it would change nothing, and the lad would still drown, she needed a third party to influence the boy and to make him change his mind. Jane found out the boy who drown was called David, and he was nine years old, he also had a friend called Simon, they had been inseparable they did everything together usually, except on that fateful day. Jane also found out that Simon also had a birthday a few days before the accident, so Jane sent a birthday card to Simon pretending to be from his aunty Betty, Simon's favorite aunt, she put in it a five-pound note and two tickets for the zoo. Valid only on the day David would have died. She also put a note in with the tickets saying these tickets are for you and your best friend David I have also arranged for you and David to have a belated birthday tea in the pavilion tea rooms inside the zoo, they are expecting you both so please don't be late. The tickets are valid only on Saturday the gates open at 9 am and your afternoon tea starts as soon as you want, have fun. Love, aunty Betty. David went with his friend to the zoo, and things did change. David grew up to be the local banker and lived a contented life. Jane, by now, was getting used to sudden visions; they happened at all times of the day or night. She did not know when a vision would come; it just did. Vision that was close to her timeline. Like and a close family relative, her vision was very vivid and strong with a sense of urgency. One such event was when her cousin Sara, aunty Charlotte's eldest, had been knocked down by a bus and suffered a broken leg and a fractured skull. The doctors feared she might have brain damage. By now Jane was getting better at getting things changed, so she phoned aunty Charlotte and told her that a new dress shop had opened uptown she should take Sara with her to have a look, Jane and her friend Sally would meet them both in Bernie's cafe for a coffee around 1 o'clock, they could catch up on old times. Sara wasn't knocked over by the bus. The bracelet never taken off, Jane began to wonder if she could Time travel whenever she wanted. She could visit relatives in the future, or off to the side branches of the family tree and reach further out along her bloodline, and she found the moonstone shone for her most nights, she could travel whenever and wherever she wanted. She could rotate the moonstone in either direction. When it clamped on the stone, she could then turn the outer ring, and depending on the direction she turned, it would send her left or right along a side branch of her family tree. In this way, she met and helped so many of her bloodline, small things and big things she was able to change and help so many of her relatives, in doing, so it made her very happy. The strangest of all so far was a vision she had. Telling her that a relative had fallen in love with a lad. That her parents did not approve of the lad. Her vision told her to somehow change the parent's attitude in favor of the lad. Jane traveled back in time, met the girl who had fallen in love, suggested that the lad should be prepared to pick up and take her parents to the hospital whenever they had an appointment. Or take

CHAPTER. 8.

them shopping in his car just to make himself useful to them. Bring the mother flowers if he was ever lucky enough to be invited to tea, in other words, show them he is not as bad as they first thought, let them know the lad doesn't smoke or drink, is in full-time employment, show them he's not a time-waster. Talk to her parents ask permission to take their daughter out to a dance or the pictures, making sure she got home on time. The Baobab tree had given Jane a vision and told her that this lad had a good heart, and he was destined to become a doctor that, during his lifetime, would help many Africans and save many many lives. So this couple did marry, and together they became missionaries and started the African foundation for hungry children, saving even more lives. Jane was particularly proud of that one. Jane perfected using the bracelet over the next few years; she found that anything she needed to know she could dream ask the tree, it never let her down. Her reply always came to her in a vision, and usually, with her next mission, needless to say, Jane was kept very busy, correcting or realigning her family's past or future. What Jane found was each time she helped to put things right, good things happened to her. She met and married the most wonderful man who loved her so much. They had two children of their own. A boy Jason and a girl Gillian who grew up and wanted to follow their mother and father helping the African people, even helping out at the African Foundation for undernourished children that had been running successfully years after its founders had passed on. Gillian took over the foundation and ran it for her lifetime, meeting and marrying a fine man who worked alongside her; they had four children and lived happily helping out in the foundation. Jane had a vision a fallen tree had crushed one of her relations. She lived with the Korowai tribe living in the Indonesian Province of Papua they were cutting down a large sago palm they used its starchy center to make it into flour then make it into bread. It served with every meal, the tree the men were cutting down twisted as it fell and hit another tree bounced off and fell into the tribe's men and women crushing a small child. And her relation, Jane time traveled back into the jungle where the tribe lived. Met the tribe's people and found them very friendly, showing Jane their way of life. How they lived as hunter-gathers. And how they gathered and harvested sago palm and process it, this was another time Jane had to use an interpreter there are over two thousand different languages on the African lands alone and over three thousand different tribes. The day of the accident. Jane took some of the children to the river close to where the accident had happened. Started to show them how to make paper boats and float them on the river, The children made such a noise laughing and jumping in after the boats, most of the tribe came to see what was making them laugh so much. At the same time, the tree was being cut down, needless to say, that accident never happened. Things went on like this for many years, and Jane's tree had started to blossom.

CHAPTER. 9

Jane's time with the bracelet was coming to an end.

She knew that her time was coming to an end when the tree produces fruit; it would be time for Jane to pass on the bracelet. She had long since let her husband into the bracelet's secrets, though she could not take him with her on her missions as Jane called them, they spent many long hours talking, who would she choose to look after the bracelet next. In the end, the tree told her in a vision to choose her son Jason as the next keeper when it became time, but the tree told her she would have time to show and to explain how things worked so that the tree and the bracelet could carry on it's blessed good work. Jane took Jason to one side, sat him down and said what I am about to show and tell you will change your life. you will have the power to change anyone of our family's past present or future. It all began with your Gr Gr Gr Grandpa Donald Rice. Then Jane spent some time telling her son Jason all about the great tree of life and how it can and will affect people in her bloodline both past, present, and future she went on to explain the ivory stones, visions, the shaman, and how the bracelet lets her time travel through time itself. We do not need to move, but I am going to take you on a trip you will never forget. With that, Jane took off her bracelet and split it in two the way that it had supposed. Gave half to Jason, who sat there wide-eyed now, please put it on. And I will show you a whole new life that you will have because as you will see, you will with the help of your tree of life and the bracelet, be able to influence the past and the future of any of our family, now close your eyes and prepare to be amazed. The tree she told Jason told me to choose you because I believe the tree has a special mission for you, it told me it has been waiting for generations for you to be born, as you are the one it tells me. But I don't know what that means, the tree will explain in your visions, She explained all about the ivory stones, the blue vase, and how to use it, how to stack the stones. She told him all about her Gr Gr Gr Grandfather Donald and how he chose her. Jane spent many days and nights teaching Jason all she knew about the ivory stones. The bracelet's powers, what the moonstones meant, and how to use and interpret the stones. Let him take apart and reassemble the bracelet just as her grandpa had shown her, and when Jane was satisfied Jason had learned as much as she could show him, she gave him the ivory stones and her lion skin bag also the blue vase that would help him find his replacement when the time comes. Then removing the bracelet for the last time, she passed it to Jason and told him to put it on. No, Jane did not die; she lived on with her husband for many years a happy and content life, because she knew things would always be OK in Jason's hands. Jason went onto help many families both in the past and in the future. Five years into his owning the bracelet, Jason had a vision that a whole village was wiped out in one night when an earthquake buried the village. Loss of life was substantial, including a family member that had married into the village. Bringing the tribe out of the hills and down to the savannah and the grasslands. Jason traveled back in time thirty years and found himself with the Chewa tribe. He needed to talk to the chief of the tribe, proving to be very difficult because Jason hadn't met the Chewa tribe before. He had to get an interpreter to be able to talk to the chief of the tribe and ask permission to enter there village, he had heard of the dispute between the Chewa and Chokwe over the grassland they both used to feed and keep cattle. Both tribes relied on their cattle not only to provide them with food but also to trade. They used cattle as marriage gifts from one family to another. Usually, from the father of the groom to the bride's father, the more cattle they gave, the higher the standing, the two families would then give the couple a dowry of say ten cows and a bull to start them off. Each member had a vested interest in the well being of all the cattle. The Chewa are part of a much larger tribe spread all over Botswana, Malawi, Mozambique, Tanzania, Zambia, and Zimbabwe. They spoke the Chichewa language. Jason was not familiar with it, so he had to use his interpreter again. The Chokwe, a much smaller tribe, also shares the grasslands and lives in Zambia. They have tribes that live in Angola, Congo (Kinshasa); they spoke only Chocwe language. Because this language Jason was not familiar with either, so once again had to use another interpreter. Both tribes lived in Zambia living just in the hills above the grasslands, both bartered with cattle as well as used them as wedding dowry. To pay for a bride or sold them to market in Kariba town south of the lands, where they fed and kept their cattle just a few miles to the north where the Zambezi river flowed. Having met and talked to the chief of the Chewa through his interpreter, Jason had found out that the other tribe's cattle were weak and skinny, this they were blaming overgrazing by the Chewa tribes cattle. As both tribes lived in the hills either side of a valley. And above the grasslands, both tribes used for grazing. Jason knew that a large earthquake in a month would completely flatten the hill and village on the Chewa side. He had met his relative who had married into the Chewa tribe. She had wed a religious man who guided the tribe through rituals and prayed to the tribe's gods that they worshipped, the god was called Chiuta, so both she and her husband highly regarded within the tribe. Jason knew he needed to save the whole village, including his family member. So Jason first went to see the grasslands and found plenty of grass to feed both tribes cattle, he went backward and forwards between both tribes and became friendly with there holy men, or witch doctors and was on friendly terms with both the tribe's chiefs. Because the chief looked to the witch doctor for guidance in any tribal disputes. Issues or rituals, Jason knew he had to befriend the

Chocwe witch doctor if he is going to have any influence with the tribe he would first need to win over the witch doctor himself. He went back to his own time and asked his own tribal shaman to give him a position that would give the Chocwe witch doctor a vision from the tree of life, asking him to listen to the white man as he had great wisdom to share, Jason went back to the Chocwe sat with the witch doctor and gave him the drink he said was the finest tonic any man could give to another, The witch doctor drank the drink and within an hour he was fast asleep, during this time he did receive a vision, believing it came from his god Chiuta, he sat with Jason and talked all about there cattle and the problems with the other tribe the Chewa, they also talked about possible solutions to the problem facing both tribes, Jason told the witch doctor I think the problem is with Chewa tribes cattle are inter breading this has made them weak, their cows are only giving birth to weak calves so maybe all they need is new blood stock, for years and years their herders have only used the bulls they have, I think it has resulted in their cattle stock becoming weaker and weaker, what they need is an infusion of new blood. Talk to your chief asked him if he would be prepared to help the other tribe by letting some of your best bulls breed with some of their cows. Improving their bloodstock and thus improving there heard. Ask your head tribesman in charge of your cattle to see if he will give his permission to let both heard intermingle. Giving both heard the freedom to bread with each other's stock will have the same effect and improve both heard. as well as making both heard a better-balanced stock with stronger cattle. In this way, it will benefit both tribes. And tell him you as chief he will hold in the highest esteem. As the one who both thought of the solution and the instigator. By bringing the tribes together in one mass celebration in peace and helping one another. your peoples will always speak about as the single most rewarding gesture ever made from one tribe to another, the ancestors of the chief will talk about it for years to come. But Jason told the witch doctor it would only work if you invite the whole Chewa village. bringing both villages together will be remembered as the most generous suggestion ever made. Tell the Chewa it must be your whole village women children old and young plus all your stock to show them you mean it, you must provide a feast with dancing and a ceremony that will last for three days. This time should coincide with midsummers day and night. Remember, tell them do not leave as much as a single animal behind. If you want it to work, your god, Chiuta, will reward you. In ways that will become apparent. Afterward? The chief of the Chewa did as his witch doctor had asked, leaving no one behind. Jason had chosen the time well because the earthquake happened as the tribe was away celebrating the joining of the cattle, not a single loss of life human or animal happened that day. Both tribes have since prospered by the joining of the cattle and still, today, let them mingle together, improving both herds. They became regarded as the finest herds on all the grasslands. The chief of the Chocwe is sung about even to this day. As the one who saved the Chewa tribe and how he helped. The bond between the tribes is so strong now, and they share everything, cattle grazing rights, even marry into each other's tribe now. The tree's prediction that Jason would be the one it had been waiting for had been filled. Though only the owners of the bracelet would ever know. Chapter. 10. Just a Few Facts about the tree of life. As well as the bark of the tree turned into clothing. The fruit, when dried naturally on the tree itself it does not need to be freeze-dried. It is 100% natural; the dried fruit is ground up and used in drinks and added to food. It has some very beneficial nutritional properties. It is a superfood; This versatile tree used for medicinal purposes by Africans across the continent. It is also famed for its incredible nutritional properties, much like the moringa, it is a superfood that deserves the name!

CHAPTER. 10.

FACTS ABOUT THE BAOBAB
TREE. THE TREE OF LIFE.

It has five times the magnesium of avocados
Four times the potassium of bananas
Twice the calcium of milk
Twice the antioxidants of acai berries, and more than any other fruit
Six times the vitamin C of oranges
Ten times the fiber of apples.
vitamin C 26.6 mg
calcium 28.5 mg
magnesium 16,1 mg
potassium 198 mg salt 0
carbohydrate 3.9 mg
sugar 3,1 mg
Fat <1

THE END.

The Baobab Tree.

ABOUT THE AUTHOR

Les Mccloskey

Now in my Seventies, I started to write books as a hobby. They are mainly for children, and I never intended to publish any. But people who read them suggested I should. So I have, up to now, I have four books published. I am not a professional writer and, the illustrations are all mine, hay they're for kids.

I hope they are enjoyed by you all. For some reason, adlults enjoy them as well.

BOOKS BY THIS AUTHOR

Mr. Mouse Needs A House.

This book is for small children, there are line drawing for coloring, and blank pages for copying.
Mr. mouse wants to marry his lady but cannot util he finds a house.

Skipping Through A Rainbow.

Samantha accidentally skips through a Rainbow, magic happens, animals begin to talk, help each other and Samantha.
Rainbows are in favor at the moment?

Simon And His Geese Story.

Simon evacuated during the way years, finds a goose shot, she leaves ten baby goslings, that Simon brings up, he trains them to respond to a sheepdog whistle.

Jane And Her Time Traveling Bracelet

Janes Gr, Gr., Grandfather travels through time and gives her the time traveling bracelet, to help family and relatives live better lives.

Printed in Poland
by Amazon Fulfillment
Poland Sp. z o.o., Wrocław